HELLO! WELCO...
FABUMOUSE WO...
THEA SiSTERS!

TheaSisters

Hi, I'm Thea Stilton, Geronimo Stilton's sister! I am a special reporter for _The Rodent's Gazette_, the most famouse newspaper on Mouse Island. I love traveling and meeting new mice all over the world, like the Thea Sisters. These five friends have helped me out with my adventures. Let me introduce you to these fabumouse young mice!

Colette has a real passion for fashion. She loves to design her own clothes in her favorite color, pink.

Violet loves studying and learning new things. She is a fan of classical music and dreams of becoming a famouse violinist someday.

Pamela loves pizza so much she eats it for breakfast. She is a skilled mechanic who can fix just about any motor she gets her paws on.

PAULINA is shy and loves to read about faraway places. But she loves traveling to those places even more.

Nicky is from the Australian Outback, where she developed a love of nature and the environment. This outdoors-loving mouse is always on the move.

Thea Sisters

Thea Stilton

MOUSEFORD ACADEMY

MICE TAKE THE STAGE

Scholastic Inc.

Copyright © 2010 by Edizioni Piemme S.p.A., Palazzo Mondadori, Via Mondadori 1, 20090 Segrate, Italy.

International Rights © Atlantyca S.p.A.

English translation © 2015 by Atlantyca S.p.A.

The publisher does not have any control over and does not assume any responsibility for author or third-party websites or their content.

GERONIMO STILTON and THEA STILTON names, characters, and related indicia are copyright, trademark, and exclusive license of Atlantyca S.p.A. All rights reserved. The moral right of the author has been asserted. Based on an original idea by Elisabetta Dami.

www.geronimostilton.com

Published by Scholastic Inc., 557 Broadway, New York, NY 10012. SCHOLASTIC and associated logos are trademarks and/or registered trademarks of Scholastic Inc.

Stilton is the name of a famous English cheese. It is a registered trademark of the Stilton Cheese Makers' Association. For more information, go to www.stiltoncheese.com.

This book is a work of fiction. Names, characters, places, and incidents are either the product of the author's imagination or are used fictitiously, and any resemblance to actual persons, living or dead, business establishments, events, or locales is entirely coincidental.

ISBN 978-0-545-87095-5

Text by Thea Stilton
Original title *La strada del successo*
Cover by Giuseppe Facciotto
Illustrations by Barbara Pellizzari and Alessandro Muscillo
Graphics by Chiara Cebraro

Special thanks to Beth Dunfey
Translated by Julia Heim
Interior design by Kay Petronio

12 11 10 9 8 7 6 5   19/0

Printed in the U.S.A.   40
First printing 2015

SNOUT IN THE CLOUDS!

It was a sunny day on Whale Island. Mouseford Academy's music class was packed with eagerly squeaking students. Professor Anna Aria had a special lesson planned for the day. She would be lecturing about popular music from around the world.

The THEA SISTERS — Colette, Nicky, Pam, Paulina, and Violet — were seated in the front row, determined not to miss a single word. But Professor Aria, who usually had her paws planted firmly on earth, seemed to have her snout in the CLOUDS!

She'd forgotten her notes in the teachers' lounge, she couldn't get the **stereo** to play, and she kept losing her train of thought.

The Thea Sisters could see their professor needed a helping paw.

FASTER than the mouse who ran up the clock, Nicky ran to get the professor's

notebook. Violet consulted her own **NOTES** and helped the professor get her lecture back on track. As for Pam, she put her magic **FIX-IT** paws to work and got the stereo working again.

"Thank you, mouselets," said Professor Aria. She tapped a few keys on her computer and told the class, "Umm, the track you're about to hear is, er, a typical example of a traditional Japanese song."

But as the first notes began to play, Paulina murmured, "Japan, my paw! This is a famouse flute song from Peru!"

The students giggled under their whiskers as the professor quickly tried to change the song. It was obvious she was more confused than a rodent in a cat kennel.

Professor Aria pulled herself together, and the lesson continued without any other problems. But as soon as they left the classroom, the Thea Sisters began chattering about their teacher.

"Professor Aria was more lost than a lab rat in a maze!" Nicky commented. "Something must be BOTHERING her."

"Hmm, I wonder," Paulina reflected. "This past week I've seen her in the computer lab a bunch of times, **typing** and *sighing*, sighing and typing . . ."

"She's distracted; she's making lots of silly mistakes . . . isn't it obvious?" Colette exclaimed. "She's got all the symptoms: Professor Aria must be **IN LOVE**! Let's go to the computer lab and get all the juicy details."

The mouselets scurried over to the lab. It was nearly empty — most students were at lunch. The only rodent seated at a

COMPUTER was Professor Aria.

The music teacher was tapping steadily on the **KEYS**. Then she cried,

"oh, my goodmouse! i can't believe it!"

Oh, my goodmouse!

A MYSTERIOUS FRIEND . . .

Alarmed, the Thea Sisters hurried to their professor's side. She was chatting with someone on the computer.

The screen **lit up** with the words: "I would like to hold our next concert on Whale Island. After all these years, **AT LAST** we'll have a chance to see each other again! What do you say?"

A **concert** on Whale Island? Who was the professor chatting with . . . and why did she seem so flustered?

Colette, Nicky, Pam, Paulina, and Violet exchanged curious **GLANCES**.

"Oh, it's nothing, mouselets," said Professor Aria, trying to **calm** down. "I'm talking to Mark Mousington, an old friend

I've just gotten back in touch with."

Colette, who was always very well informed, twitched her tail. "Mark Mousington? You mean the producer of the mouserrific **RATSTREET BOYS**?"

The other mouselets stood there with their snouts hanging open like a pack of hungry cats at feeding time. The Ratstreet Boys were the hottest band on Mouse Island!

"Yes, him," Professor Aria admitted with a SMILE. "We grew up together. We've been FRIENDS since we were mouselings."

The professor pulled an old PHOTO out of her pocket. It

showed a young mouselet holding a guitar. Her snout was full of **JOY** and **HOPE**, and she was smiling broadly. Next to her was a young mouse with a crazy fur-do and a funny outfit. He was looking at her *tenderly*. It was the professor and Mark Mousington, many years earlier!

"We were close **friends** who shared a love of music. When we turned fifteen, we

started our first **band**," Professor Aria **EXPLAINED**. "We played small shows whenever and wherever we could. It was so much fun to go through it all **together** . . ."

"And then what happened?" Violet asked. The professor's snout turned sad. "One day a famouse agent contacted me about a role in a musical directed by Professor Ratyshnikov. It was a great honor, and they really wanted me. So I left, and **unfortunately** Mark and I fell out of touch. But over the years, I've followed his career as a producer. And now we've found each other again thanks to the INTERNET."

Just then, a new message from Mousington flashed on-screen. "Everything okay? If there's a problem, I can hold the concert someplace else . . ."

Professor Aria reflected for a moment. Then she typed: "We would be happy to host you and the Ratstreet Boys at Mouseford!"

The mouselets were so EXCITED, they couldn't help squeaking loudly.

The professor's old pal was still typing. He had another idea. The Ratstreet Boys needed an opening act for their show, and Mousington wanted to **CHOOSE** a band from among the students at Mouseford! He suggested holding a contest to see who'd get to open the show.

"What a fabumouse idea!" cried Colette. She and the other Thea Sisters were happier than a pack of mouselings on their first trip to Luck E. Cheez. A concert by their favorite musical group, plus an exciting new challenge to face **together**!

Her students' **excitement** made Professor Aria smile. Then her expression turned thoughtful. She wondered what it would be like to see her childhood friend again after so many years . . .

Cheese niblets!

Hooray, the Ratstreet Boys!

PAM'S PREDICAMENT

Professor Ratyshnikov and the other professors in the art, music, and theater department were enthusiastic about hosting a Ratstreet Boys concert, especially when they heard about the contest. It was a fantastic opportunity for their students to practice and perform live!

The **AUDITIONS** were set for the end of the week, when the Ratstreet Boys would be on the island. News of the contest spread through the halls of the academy **FASTER** than the smell of melting cheese. Nearly every mouse at Mouseford decided to participate.

RUBY FLASHYFUR, who was always ready to take center stage, told everyone she knew Mark Mousington very well. "Winning this contest is going to be easier than taking a cheese pop from a mouseling!" she boasted to her friends, the Ruby Crew.

Meanwhile, Mouseford's other students were seriously **GETTING ORGANIZED**. The moment

the Thea Sisters had heard about the contest, they'd decided to form a group. They met in the **LIZARD CLUB** common room to plan their act.

"The five of us are very **close**," Nicky observed. "And we each know how to sing or play an instrument. Mouselets, we're practically a **BAND** already!"

"I think I could write a **song** for us to play," Violet said timidly.

"I'll play the guitar," Nicky continued.

Paulina clapped her paws. "My synthesizer can provide all the backup instruments we need. It'll sound as if we have a **full** orchestra behind us!"

"Yesssssss!" cheered Colette. "And I could sing!"

"Um, I guess I'll play . . . umm . . . I'll play . . ." Pam muttered.

Then she scratched her snout. "Oh, *mumbling mufflers*, mouselets! I don't know what I could possibly play."

Her **friends** gathered around her, suggesting various options.

"You can be our **backup singer**, Pam!"

"No, we absolutely need a **SAXOPHONE**!"

"Why don't you try the **triangle**?"

"Thanks, sisters, but I don't think we're following the right strand of string cheese . . ." Pam said thoughtfully.

BACKUP SINGER?

HMM, THAT'S NOT REALLY UP HER ALLEY!

THE SAXOPHONE?

NOPE, NOT HER STYLE!

THE TRIANGLE?

NOT ROCKIN' ENOUGH!

What a predicament! A band without Pam was out of the question: the Thea Sisters all agreed on that.

For a moment, the mouselets thought about **GIVING UP**. But Pam wouldn't hear of it.

"I'll figure it out, I promise. Why don't you grab your **INSTRUMENTS** and start getting ready? I'll meet you in the practice room in a little while."

So the group went their separate ways, and Pam stayed alone, **tHiNKiNG**.

If I could only play the monkey wrench! she reflected, smiling ruefully.

A BREWING STORM

Professor Aria was determined to encourage all her aspiring rock stars. She left different musical instruments in the school's rehearsal rooms for the students to try out.

Violet was the Thea Sisters' resident music expert. She immediately began setting up for **BAND** practice in her favorite practice room.

When Nicky and Paulina entered the room, they found Violet waiting there with a copy of the MUSICAL ARRANGEMENT for each of them. The melody was really lovely, and the mouselets began practicing at once.

"Careful, Nicky," Violet said as she listened to her friends practice. "The harmony

changes here — it's easy to miss."

Then she turned to Paulina, who was playing violin chords on her synthesizer. "Wait, I'm not sure about that! Let's try wind instead of strings. But . . . one second. Where's Colette?"

Right then, Colette burst into the room. "Sorry, mouselets! I got stuck in math class —"

"You're here at last!" Violet interrupted. "Come on, we've been waiting for you."

The whole time the Thea Sisters practiced,

Let's get to work!

Violet paced nervously among them, giving them tips on how to improve their playing. But as hard as Nicky, Paulina, and Colette tried, they couldn't get the right sound. Their music seemed out of tune and **OFFBEAT**!

That wasn't surprising: the mouselets were all so afraid of messing up that each one was **CONCENTRATING** too hard on her own part. They'd forgotten to listen to one another, so there was no harmony. They sounded **worse** than cat claws on a chalkboard!

"That's enough, mouselets!" Violet finally *blurted out*. "This is not the melody I wrote for our group."

"We're trying our best, Vi," Nicky replied. She was feeling tired and **grouchy** after their long practice.

Colette nodded in **exhaustion**. "Nicky's right, we need more time to practice."

"It's the first time we've played this piece," Paulina added, trying to be tactful. "We're trying our best, and that's more important than playing perfectly."

Violet was stunned. Perhaps she had been too harsh with her friends, but music required discipline!

"But . . . but . . ." she managed to stutter. "We have to keep WORKING if we want to get it right. I'm doing this for the group! Don't you UNDERSTAND?"

"Vi, we know we aren't as good as you," Nicky said. "But that's why we need to work TWICE as hard! And your criticism is making us nervous."

"I'm not criticizing, I'm just trying to help you play better," Violet insisted. "Music REQUIRES sacrifice, hard work, and commitment!"

"That's true, but it also requires JOY, passion, and ENTHUSIASM," Colette interrupted. "And, to be honest, you're taking all the fun out of it!"

I'm leaving!

Violet recoiled in shock. "Well, then maybe you'll be better off **without me**!"

And she $JUMPED$ UP and scurried out of the practice room.

Her friends **watched** her go, but they didn't try to stop her.

The Thea Sisters' first band practice had ended in a **fight**!

DRUMROLL, PLEASE!

At that very moment, unaware of her friends' troubles, Pam was wandering around trying to figure out how she could fit into the band. The academy's HaLLWaYS were deserted — all the students were busy practicing.

All . . . or almost all! Suddenly, the mouselets' friend Elly Squid popped out of a classroom. "Hey, Pam!"

"Hi, Elly," Pam replied with a sad smile. "Why aren't you preparing for Mark Mousington's auditions?"

"Oh, don't even squeak that name to me!" Elly moaned. "Craig, Tanja, and I want to form a group, but there isn't enough TIME to practice. How about you and the other Thea Sisters?"

Pam shook her snout sadly. "If only it were a dance competition — I've got some awesome HiP-HOP moves!" she said. "But I don't have the chops to play a musical instrument."

As she was squeaking, Pam beat one paw on the wall next to her.

Tippetty-tappetty-tip!

"I just can't think of any instrument that's right for me," she went on, knocking her paws lightly against the wall.

Tippety-tappety-tip-tip-tap!

Elly's snout lit up. "Actually, I think I know just the instrument for you. Come on, Pam!"

Without waiting for her friend to answer, she took Pam by the paw and dragged her into town. Soon they'd reached the Thrifty Rat, the store Elly's sisters ran.

Elly led Pam into the storage room, which was **cluttered** with objects: hatboxes, irons, a rocking chair, velvet armchairs, a gramophone, a pair of old skis . . .

"You can find almost anything at the Thrifty Rat!" Pam said as she looked around.

Elly nodded. "Yeah, that's why we're here. Look!" She led Pam to a bulky shape covered with a **LARGE** white cloth.

I have! an idea

TAPTAP

25

Elly whipped off the sheet, revealing the most beautiful drum set Pam had ever seen. It was **bright** red, with yellow flames. It seemed a bit worn, but otherwise, it was **PERFECT**!

"Jumping gerbil babies, that's a sweet set of skins!" exclaimed Pam, her eyes sparkling.

You see, Pam had always loved the **DRUMS**. When she was a wee mouseling, she used to put on concerts using pots and pans with a spoon as her drumstick!

"You're a genius, Elly!" Pam said, hugging her. "Why didn't I think of this before?"

"My dad is devoted to these drums," Elly explained. "When he finds out it's for a friend, I'm sure he'll be **happy** to lend them to you."

Pam got comfortable behind the set and unleashed a lively drumroll.

Tippetty-tappetty-tip-tip-tip-tap-TIP!

A BIG MESS!

When Pam got back to Mouseford, the sun was **SETTING**. On the horizon, the sea was lit up all golden and **red**.

She hurried to the practice room to tell her friends about the INCREDIBLE discovery that she'd made in the Thrifty Rat storage room. She had no idea what kind of glue trap she was about to get stuck in.

"Hey, mouselets!" Pam exclaimed. "I have some fabumouse news!"

Then she stopped and **LOOKED** around in confusion. Nicky was sadly strumming a few **NOTES** on her guitar, while Colette and Paulina were wearily **scribbling** in their notebooks. **Crumpled** balls of paper covered with *cross outs* surrounded them.

"Hey!" Pam said. "Why the long snouts? And where's Vi?"

"Oh, Pam, thank goodmouse you're back!" Colette *exclaimed*. "We've been practicing for hours, but Violet told us we're not good enough. She kept pacing around, CRITICIZING us. We all got really stressed, and we FOUGHT like cats

Mouselets, I think I've got it!

Pam, thank goodmouse you're back!

and rats, and now we don't know what to do!"

Pam was shocked. Nicky and Paulina quickly filled her in on all the trouble they'd had during practice.

"We've been trying to come up with some **GOOD LYRICS** for the song to convince Violet to come back," said Paulina, pointing to the crumpled papers on the ground.

Sigh...

"We've been at it for hours, but we haven't come up with anything decent."

"What a **cat-astrophe**!" Pam cried.

Just then, Shen's snout peeked around the door. "Hey! How's the first **band practice** going?" he asked. A quick look at his friends was all it took for him to realize something was off.

"Hmm, you mice look sleepier than Santa Mouse the day after Christmas," he said, trying to cheer them up. "It's been a long day for everyone. A good **NIGHT'S** rest will get you back on your paws."

The mouselets decided to take his advice. Yawning, they **headed** for the door.

"You're right, Shen," admitted Nicky. "Right now I'm grouchier than a groundhog. We need to rest a bit, and then we'll get our brains in 𝐠𝐞𝐚𝐫."

Paulina nodded. "Tomorrow we'll figure out how to get Violet back."

Shen watched as the Thea Sisters scampered off. Then his gaze fell on the papers the mouselets had THROWN AWAY. He read a few lines and smiled. "Of course you'll figure it out, and perhaps I can lend a paw!"

A TELLING TALE

NIGHT fell on Whale Island. At Mouseford Academy, not a student was stirring, except for one mouse . . . Violet! After the **FIGHT** with her friends, she had scurried back to her room.

She was very **upset**. The band needed someone who knew music . . . why didn't the other mouselets understand?

What happened?

But when Violet calmed down, she realized she'd been **bossier** than a beaver building a dam. The most important thing wasn't to sound like a professional band but to have fun jamming with her friends.

"This is awful! I've got to fix things right away," she said to herself.

Violet sprang to her paws, put on her bathrobe, and picked up her BELOVED violin. Playing always helped cheer her up — and helped her think. She headed to the school's soundproof practice room.

When Violet opened the door, the notes of a romantic MELODY wafted out. Seated at the PiANO was Professor Aria.

"Violet!" the teacher exclaimed. "What are you doing here at this hour . . . and with your violin?"

"Oh, I needed to relax and reflect a bit," Violet answered.

Professor Aria nodded in understanding. "Yes, I'm the same way. I hide away to play whenever I need to think. So tell me, what's BOTHERING you?"

Violet really needed a friend, so she told her professor about her argument with the other Thea Sisters.

Professor Aria listened attentively. Then

she said, "Music and friendship are two precious gifts. But they don't always mix." She beckoned Violet to sit next to her.

"When Mark and I were little, music was everything for us."

Professor Aria went on. "Every afternoon we would meet to play, and we'd spend HOURS talking about new songs."

The professor picked up the TUNE she'd been playing when Violet had come in. "This is the last song we ever wrote together. We called it 'The Road to Success.' It was a road we hoped to travel down together."

"What happened?" Violet asked.

Her teacher sighed. "Back then, we were both GROWING as musicians, and each of us wanted to force our ideas on the other. So our simple, spontaneous friendship suddenly became COMPLiCATeD."

The professor's tale reminded Violet of the miscommunication between her and her friends.

"One day we argued right before a concert," the professor recalled. "I had a new idea about how to finish 'The Road to Success,' but Mark didn't like it.

"We went onstage SULKING like squirrels. We wouldn't even look at each other! After the show, an agent asked me to go on tour."

Violet gazed at the professor. She seemed so SAD!

"I was still MAD at Mark, so I said yes right away," Professor Aria concluded. "The next day I called him, but the way he squeaked to me was colder than iced cheese.

Hmph!

You're not listening to me!

"He just said 'good luck' and hung up! But if he had asked me to stay, I never would have LEFT."

The professor's story really moved Violet. "So your friendship ended because of a song?"

"First we stopped listening to each other, and then we stopped talking, and then we just avoided each other," Professor Aria said. "Your friends were trying to tell you something today, but maybe you weren't really **LISTENING** to them. Or am I wrong?"

"No, you're right, Professor," Violet said. "I was so busy trying to get them to **LISTEN** to me, I couldn't hear what they were trying to tell me."

Violet stood up. "Well, it's time to scrape the cheese out of my ears. I've got to squeak with my friends at once. And this time, I'm going to **listen** to them!"

THE SPICE MICE!

That **NIGHT**, Pamela couldn't sleep, either. So she got up in the dark and tiptoed down the academy's **deserted** hallways.

"**Thank goodmouse** for my secret stash of Cheesy Chews!" she murmured as she slipped into the **LIZARD CLUB'S** common room. She was about to open the pantry when a pale white snout appeared before her.

Eeeeeeek!

Pam nearly jumped out of her fur.

The mysterious figure let out a **SNICKER**.

"C-Colette! Is that you?" Pam stammered.

It was. Her friend stood before her in a pink nightgown,

POM-POM slippers, and a yogurt mask slathered all over her snout.

"When I'm feeling **anxious**, a beauty treatment is the only thing that calms me down, you know that," Colette explained, grinning.

"I needed a little pick-me-up, too," Pam said, snacking on a Cheesy Chew.

The two friends headed back to their room paw in paw.

In the HALLWAY, they ran into Nicky, who was leaving the GYM. "Working out always helps me clear my mind," she explained.

The three mouselets headed to the COMPUTER lab in search of Paulina. Sure enough, she was there, bent over a computer.

Once the four mouselets had REUNITED, they decided they couldn't wait till morning to talk to Violet. They needed to find her *immediately* and convince her to come back to the band, even if it meant dragging her out of bed by her tail!

As soon as they left the LAB, they ran

right into Violet and Professor Aria.

The five mouselets stared at one another squeaklessly. Then they burst out laughing. They were a totally **ridicumouse** sight, some of them in pajamas and slippers, and all of them unable to sleep!

Violet scurried into her friends' paws, sobbing, "Oh, I'm sorry, mouselets! I acted more conceited than a cat!"

"It wasn't you, Vi," Paulina cried.

Nicky nodded. "We were the unfair ones!"

Colette agreed. "You were just trying to help us . . ."

The misunderstanding had brought the THEA SISTERS closer together than ever.

Professor Aria smiled. "You rodents CARe about one another so much; I can tell you'll make a really GREAT band."

"Yeah! We're more than friends; we're sisters — sisters who rock!" Paulina exclaimed. "In fact, that should be our band name! The Rock Sisters."

"Hmm . . . I think we need to spice it up a bit," said Pam.

"Spice . . . that's it!" cried Nicky. "Let's call ourselves the **Spice Mice**!"

"I love it! It's the perfect name for our band," Violet agreed.

"Yesss!" the others exclaimed, gathering **around** her.

The peace was made, and a new band was born!

STUCK-UP
SUPERSTARS

The next morning, Mouseford's headmaster, Octavius de Mousus, all the teachers, and a **CROWD** of fans gathered at Mouse Island's heliport to greet the Ratstreet Boys.

The Thea Sisters were in the front row. They were more **EXCITED** than a pack of hungry mice at an all-you-can-eat cheese buffet.

Shen was the last to arrive. He **scurried** toward the mouselets with a stack of **papers** in his paw.

"Hey, you're late!" Ryder Flashyfur called over to him. "Are all

Huff, huff

those papers for autographs?"

Shen shook his snout. "No, it's lyrics for the Thea Sisters' song. It took me all **NIGHT** to write this."

"Aw, that's nice of you. I heard they had a hard time yesterday. It's gotta be better than what they were working on," Ryder said.

At that moment, the Ratstreet Boys' helicopter landed. The crowd burst into applause.

Clap! Clap! Clap! Clap!

Professor Aria saw her old friend was about to disembark. Her *heart* was beating faster than a gerbil on a wheel.

"Welcome to Mouseford Academy, Mark," she managed to say, shaking his paw.

Mousington **MUTTERED** a thank-you and then **STARED** at her awkwardly. For a moment, it felt as if they were the only

Umm . . . welcome to Mouseford, Mark!

Th-thanks!

two rodents on the island.

Suddenly, the murmur of the crowd became an **UPROAR**: the Ratstreet Boys were stepping out of the helicopter!

Four ratlets appeared at the door to the helicopter, looking bored.

They all put on their **DARK SUNGLASSES** at the same time.

Bud, the guitarist, came down first. He immediately began complaining, "Here we

So awesome!
Go, Ratstreet Boys!
THE RATSTREET BOYS
LEGENDARY
THE RATSTREET BOYS
You rock

are in nowheresville again . . ."

"Yeah," agreed Raven, the bassist, tossing his blond fur.

"And the same old CROWD of screaming mouselets . . ." added Jamal, the lead singer.

Joel, the group's drummer, a mouse with curly fur, was the last one down the stairs. He waved to the crowd.

Jamal put his paw on the headmaster's shoulder. "Yo, this place is a bore. Where can a mouse find some FUN around here?"

The Thea Sisters were right next to the stairs. They'd heard every word, and they couldn't believe their ears.

"These are the musicians we're such huge fans of?" Violet said.

"That's no way to treat their fans, or their hosts!" Nicky exclaimed, shaking her snout.

Colette was the most disappointed. "And to think I have all their albums," she sighed. "Why, I know all the words to 'Quit Playing Tricks (With My Tail)!'"

But while the Thea Sisters had changed their **MINDS** about the band, someone else thought their behavior was **A-OK**: Ruby Flashyfur! A big smile spread across her snout as she scurried over to Mark Mousington and invited him and the band to a party on her mother's yacht.

Sure, we'll come . . .

The four ratlets accepted the invitation **IMMEDIATELY**!

But Mark Mousington was **less excited**.

"Sure, we'll come, thanks," he confirmed.

But then he added, "As long as Anna and the other professors are there, too."

Ruby's smile DISAPPEARED like cheddar into a cheese grater. She wanted to convince the producer to pick her and her friends as the opening band for the Ratstreet Boys. With the professors under paw, it would be a lot harder to **influence** his decision!

As for Professor Aria, she couldn't wait to spend some time with Mark. Her old friend's request made her whiskers tingle: maybe their friendship wasn't lost after all!

A Rockin' Rival

After the welcome *ceremony*, the Thea Sisters hurried over to the rehearsal ROOM to practice. But first Pam stopped by her SUV to pick up the drum set she'd borrowed from Elly's father.

The last thing she expected was to find someone waiting there for her. It was Joel, the Ratstreet Boys' drummer!

"Hey, is this your drum kit?" the ratlet asked her, pointing to the **instrument** in the back of her **CAR**.

"Er, yes. Well, actually, I borrowed it from a friend," Pam replied. "Isn't it nice?"

"Yeah! It's got a great look," said Joel. "My name's Joel."

"Um, I know," Pam mumbled, blushing. "I'm Pam."

"Looks like you've got good taste in cars, too!" Joel said, nodding at her car.

The two rodents began chatting. It turned out Joel had a great sense of humor, plus a deep love of cars *and* drums!

After they'd been squeaking happily for a few minutes, Pam asked, "So, um, don't you need to get back to the rest of the band?"

Joel sighed. "Yes, probably. I love hanging

Let me give you a few tips!

Awesome, thanks!

out with the guys, but I can't stand the crowds." He grinned at her. "Tell me about you and your friends. Are you going to PARTICIPATE in the contest?" When Pam said yes, he gave her a bunch of great tips.

After they finally said good-bye, Pam couldn't help smiling. *Joel doesn't seem as snooty as the other members of the group!* she reflected, *pleasantly* surprised.

The mouselet didn't realize there was

someone watching them from afar with a 𝕤𝕒𝕕 expression on his snout. It was Shen! He had a little **CRUSH** on Pam, and when he saw her hanging out with a famouse musician, he couldn't help feeling a **TWINGE** of jealousy.

"That's the drummer from the Ratstreet Boys," he mumbled. "What chance does my SILLY song have with Pam when she's hanging out with rock stars?"

He crumpled up the paper he'd written his song on and tossed it away. Then he scurried off, dragging his tail behind him.

Ryder happened to be crossing campus at that same moment. He noticed his friend and picked up the crumpled paper CURIOUSLY. He quickly scanned it, and a strange gleam lit up his green eyes. Then he carefully folded the paper and PUT IT in his pocket.

BEAUTY-SHOP PRACTICE

That afternoon, the Thea Sisters' practice began to pay off. They were starting to sound like a real **BAND**. Pam let loose on the drums, and Nicky held her own on the guitar.

Paulina and Violet accompanied them on

the COMPUTER and KEYBOARD.
"Spice Mice, we sound smooth, like cream cheese on a bagel!" Pam said, clapping her paws HAPPILY.

The only one who didn't share her enthusiasm was Colette. She was warming up her squeak, but she didn't have any lyrics to sing!

"Well, I tried!" Pam protested. That

morning, she'd shown the mouselets a few lyrics she'd come up with.

"Yes, your LYRICS were . . . interesting," Violet said tactfully.

Nicky was more direct. "The Spice Mice need something more relatable than, 'Roaring engines from above, you are my one and only love!'"

"Love!" Colette EXCLAIMED. "That's the answer: we'll write a love song!"

Paulina pointed to the pink papers that Colette had scattered around the practice room. "We already tried that . . ." She picked up a piece of paper and read it: "'My heart's beating faster than a hamster on a wheel, I think you'd better call the doctor for real.'"

The mouselets looked at one another. Then they all burst into giggles.

"Yeah, we can't perform in front of Mark Mousington with lyrics like that," Colette admitted. "We'll get laughed offstage!"

Meanwhile, the Ruby Crew — Ruby Flashyfur and her friends Alicia, Connie, and Zoe — was having problems, too. To prepare for the party that evening, Ruby had transformed her room into a beauty salon. She'd forced her friends to keep practicing while a bevy of beauticians COMBED their fur and applied their makeup.

"Careful, mouselets: the lead singer's squeak has to rise above all the others!" yelled Ruby, waving a furbrush around.

"Just when did we decide that you would be the lead singer?" Connie demanded.

Ruby *glared* at her. "Why, I believe it was when you agreed to audition with the amazing song that my mom had the best composers **write**!"

"Of course, of course," Zoe said quickly. "But learning a song under these conditions is harder than finding a cheese slice in a haystack!"

"I wish we didn't have to practice under these **FUR DRYERS**," Alicia added. "I can't

Our act has to be perfect, got it?!

even hear the sound of my own squeak!"

"What difference does that make?" Ruby SNICKERED, sticking her snout in the air.

"Most record contracts get signed at parties, not in rehearsal rooms! It doesn't matter how we sound, it's all about the LOOK. And tonight we're going to look great! This party is our ticket to the ENTERTAINMENT world."

Connie and Zoe agreed, but Alicia wasn't so sure. "Maybe, but I heard the Thea Sisters are practicing really hard!"

Ruby stopped smiling. The mention of the Thea Sisters rubbed her fur the wrong way. "Oh, yeah? Well, I can be serious, too!" she hissed. "And soon everyone will realize that!"

She grabbed her cell phone and stormed out.

A MAGICAL EVENING?

The sun had **set**, and Mouseford Academy's lights were turning on one by one when the Thea Sisters **finally** finished with band practice.

"Okay, sisters, time to **KICK UP** our paws," Nicky said. "Our sound is totally rockin'."

Colette nodded. "But we still need the words . . ."

An elegant **SHADOW** swept toward them from down the hallway. It was accompanied by the rhythmic clicking of high heels.

CLIP-CLOP-CLIP-CLOP!

The mouselets were squeakless: it was Professor Aria, in a dark **silk** gown with an embroidered top and a red sash. She looked absolutely fabumouse!

"You're so *ELEGANT*, Professor!" Violet said **ADMIRINGLY**.

"Thank you!" Professor Aria responded, out of BREATH. "And I'm also very late!"

Violet thought about Professor Aria's story. She knew how **EXCITED** their teacher was to catch up with Mark after so many years.

Hi, mouselets!

"It's going to be an **amazing** evening!" she said kindly, smiling at Professor Aria.

The Thea Sisters walked the professor to

the academy's main door, where a TAXI was waiting to take her to the port.

"How romantic!" Colette sighed, her blue eyes sparkling. "She looks like she just stepped out of a fairy tale!"

"And Mark will be her handsome prince . . ." Violet concluded dreamily.

But as Professor Aria headed toward the port, Ruby Flashyfur was waiting on her mother's yacht with a SURPRISE that was not magical at all.

You see, Ruby was desperate to get Mark Mousington to squeak with her. But she was about to give up: the producer was too distracted even to LOOK at her! He was pacing nervously back and forth.

He looked awkward in his elegant suit, and he wouldn't stop glancing over at the yacht's gangplank.

Ruby was wound up TIGHTER than a mousetrap spring. She knew the producer must be waiting for Professor Aria! He had been so insistent that she be invited to the party.

Well, if Mark was interested in the professor, she'd get his ATTENTION by talking about her. "Professor Aria has told me a lot about your friendship," the mouselet said with a FAKE smile.

"Really?" Mousington ASKED, suddenly interested. "What did she say?"

Ruby immediately began to spin a wild tale, trying to make Professor Aria look worse than a hunk of moldy mozzarella.

"Well, I don't like to say anything bad about anyone, but . . ." she whispered, "the professor told me that between the two of you, she was the one who really knew how to play music!"

Mark Mousington was taken aback. "What?!"

Ruby had managed to **PROVOKE** him! But she had no time to celebrate the success of her tricky paw-pulling. Mousington stalked off and stood brooding in a corner for the rest of the evening.

A DELICIOUS
EVENING OUT

After dinner, the Thea Sisters met up with their classmates in the Lizard Club common room. Suddenly, in the **middle** of their conversation, Pam's cell phone began to ring. BRRIiing! BRRIiing!

"Who can that be at this hour?" the mouselet muttered. Then she looked at her phone's DISPLAY, and her tail stiffened.

It was Joel, the drummer from the Ratstreet Boys! Pam had given him her NUMBER that afternoon, but she never expected that he'd actually call her!

In fact, Joel had been waiting for the

chance to call all EVENING. He'd finally sneaked out of the yacht party, which he'd found more boRing than a trip to Ho-Hum Island.

It wasn't every day he got to meet a cute, funny mouselet who shared his love of CARS and DRUMS, and he couldn't wait to see her again.

Pam invited Joel to meet her and the other Thea Sisters at the **ice-cream** parlor in the port, and he eagerly accepted.

When the mouselets got to the pier, they saw Professor Aria scurrying off the yacht and jumping into a **TAXI**. The professor waved at them, but they could tell **right away** that something was wrong: that wasn't the professor's usual **RADIANT** smile!

"She couldn't wait to leave, either," Joel explained. "She spent all evening **CIRCLING** Ruby like a rat sniffing a crusty chunk of cheese!"

Joel continued his story as they **scampered** into town. The more he talked, the more the Thea Sisters **UNDERSTOOD** why Professor Aria was so upset. Mark Mousington had turned his tail on her all night long. He didn't invite her to dance even once, and every time she tried to squeak with him, he talked to someone else. What a **disappointment** for their teacher, who had been so excited to see him again!

After their ice-cream cones, it was time for the mouselets to return to school. Joel offered to walk them back to campus. He and Pam scurried along behind the others, **chatting** about anything and everything.

Pam felt like she'd met her dream ratlet, but there was **DISAPPOINTMENT** in store for her, too.

"After this concert, I'm going to Europe for a few weeks to relax and find inspiration," Joel said. "You should come with me."

Pam turned **PINKER** than a cat's nose, but she shook her snout. "Oh, thanks, but I can't. You know, I have exams here at school, plus a **presentation** I'm working on with the other Thea Sisters."

Joel stared at her in **ASTONISHMENT**. "Exams! Pam, has the cheese slipped off your cracker? You've got to seize the moment. Don't waste your time on tests!"

Pam was **TAKEN ABACK**. "But

I'm going to Europe ...

school is important to me! Plus, I promised my friends we'd do this project together."

"So you'd give up the chance of a lifetime for your friends?" Joel **teased** her.

Suddenly, Pam realized she and Joel were as DIFFERENT as cheddar and Camembert. "My friends, my family — they are my life," she said, brushing him off. "They count on me, and I know I can always count on them. GOOD NIGHT!"

She scampered away, leaving Joel staring after her. *What a strange mouselet!*

MUCH MORE THAN A SONG

The next day, Mark Mousington and the Ratstreet Boys visited the **ACADEMY**. The headmaster proudly led them on a tour of the **HALLWAYS** and classrooms.

Professor Aria trailed along after them. She was totally down in the snout.

Mark Mousington **watched** her **DESPONDENTLY**. He knew he'd messed up the night before, but he didn't know how to fix it!

Pam was in a **bad mood**, too. She was stewing over Joel's behavior, and she spent the whole tour staring into **space**. Colette, Nicky, Paulina, and Violet didn't know where to look.

Between Pam's **long** snout and

Professor Aria's **aloof** attitude, the morning seemed to stretch on longer than a strand of string cheese!

It was a relief when the Thea Sisters were finally able to break away and go to the rehearsal room. There a strange **surprise** awaited them.

Violet picked up a sheet of paper next to the **microphone** and read it aloud:

I don't want to talk to him!

"'Thea Sisters, this song is for you. Please feel free to use my words. They are yours because you were their inspiration.'"

"Wow!" squeaked Colette. "We haven't even been a band for a full week, and we already have our first fan!"

The lyrics described a mouselet who was full of life, an expert on engines who overcame obstacles with a smile on her snout.

Mouserific!

Come on!

Everyone turned toward Pam, who turned **redder** than a cheese rind. "Are y-you saying someone wrote this about me?"

Paulina took the paper and scurried over to her synthesizer. "Listen up! The chorus is perfect for our **SONG**."

As she played, two unexpected listeners lurked outside: Ryder and Shen, who'd come

by to see how practice was going.

"B-but . . . that's my song!" Shen froze like a fish stick. "How did they . . . ?" Then he turned and saw Ryder giggling under his WHISKERS.

"It's a really great **song**," the ratlet confessed. "I couldn't let you throw it away."

Ryder had been waiting for the right moment to bring Shen by to say hello. He'd timed it perfectly.

"Shen! Guess what?" Nicky greeted him. "We found the perfect lyrics for our song!"

Ryder lingered outside in the hallway, waiting to enjoy the moment of revelation. But what he heard next threw mold all over his cheesecake.

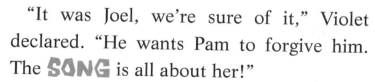

"It was Joel, we're sure of it," Violet declared. "He wants Pam to forgive him. The **SONG** is all about her!"

The mouselets gathered around Pam, who still wasn't totally convinced.

As for Shen, he was quiet as a mouse. He was way too *shy* to tell them the truth!

AUDITIONS, WITH A SIDE OF SABOTAGE!

The contest **AUDITIONS** began the next day. The jury entered the auditorium and took their seats in the **FRONT ROW**. Mark Mousington sat next to Professor Aria, who wouldn't even **LOOK** at him.

Guest judges Professor Ratyshnikov and Headmaster de Mousus **came in** right

behind them. Then the Ratstreet Boys filed in and took seats behind the professors.

The schedule for the tryouts was posted outside the theater. Onstage, behind the **curtain**, the first bands began to prepare.

Pam found the Spice Mice's name on the list. "We're up in a little bit," she told her friends. "We're the fourth band."

"All right, let's *HAUL TAIL*!" Violet said. "We have to set up our instruments."

But when the mouselets reached their rehearsal room, they were in for a real shock. Pam's drums, Paulina's synthesizer, Nicky's guitar, and all the other instruments had DISAPPEARED!

"Wh-what happened to our instruments?" Paulina cried.

A smug squeak came from the doorway.

"Oooh, what a tragedy! Now how will you participate in the tryouts?"

It was Ruby. She'd shown up in the fur to check on her **wicked** sabotage!

"Ruby! You're as sneaky as a snake in the grass," said Pam, scowling. "I'll bet you know all about this mysterious disappearance, don't you?"

Before Ruby could respond, her cell phone rang.

"Don't let me interrupt your panic attacks, mouselets," Ruby said snidely. "I've simply GOT TO take this call!"

She scampered off in a flash.

Her personal assistant, Alan, was on the other end of the line.

"Ruby, I took the instruments like you *told* me to," Alan began. "Then I loaded them in a truck, but . . . umm, what do I do with them now? Where do you want me to take them?"

"*I don't know and I don't care!*" Ruby replied. "Hide them somewhere and then **unload** them in the town square. The important thing is that the Thea Sisters don't find them until the auditions are over . . . got it?!"

THIS ISN'T OVER!

"Putrid cheese puffs," Pam **BURST OUT**. "Having our instruments stolen at the last minute . . . what a nightmare! It's like trying to compete in a MOUSCAR race without a gas pedal!"

The mouselets looked at one another despairingly. After all their hard work, the arguing, the endless practicing . . . it was so unfair to have to **GIVE UP**!

Here's the answer!

But Paulina wasn't going out without a fight. "This isn't over yet!" she announced, waving a **CD** in front of her friends. "Guess what? I recorded our music on this. I just need to borrow a **COMPUTER** to add the accompaniment . . . and I know just who to ask!"

Professor Van Kraken, the mouselets' marine biology professor, had recently purchased a *new* synthesizer to reproduce the sounds of MARINE animals.

"It's different from mine," Paulina admitted. "But I should be able to work on it! I just need a bit of time . . ."

"If only we had TIME; it's our turn in a minute," Nicky groaned.

"Sisters, sometimes you gotta break a few eggs to make a cheesecake. I'll go convince Mark Mousington to move us to the end of the LIST," Colette declared.

"All right, Coco!" Violet said. A tiny bit of hope lit up her snout. "And I'll ask Elly's group if we can borrow their guitar and keyboard."

"And I'm sure Joel will lend me his **drum set**," Pam put in. "Since he helped us with our song lyrics, I'm sure he'd be willing to help us again. What do you say, mouselets?"

"I say it sounds like a plan!" Paulina declared.

"THEA SISTERS, let's get to work!" Colette concluded. "There's no time to lose!"

The mouselets split up, each one with a *mission* to carry out.

Let's get to work!

Colette headed to the **auditorium** to find Mark Mousington. Could she convince him to change the schedule and let the Spice Mice play last?

She found the producer pacing nervously up and down the **HALLS**. He was upset about the misunderstanding with Professor Aria. The long years of separation had been real **TORTURE** for him, and now that he'd found his long-lost friend, he couldn't bear the idea of losing her again.

Colette approached, introduced herself, and **BRIEFLY** explained the situation. "So would you let us play last?"

Mousington immediately felt sympathy for the mouselet. He also felt as if he had known her for years, but that couldn't be possible, could it?

"Of course," he exclaimed. "You must be

May I squeak with you?

Colette from the Thea Sisters. Anna has told me so much about you. You're one of her most promising students!"

Colette bLuSHeD to the roots of her fur. "She's told us about you, too, and about how you began playing music **together**. She remembers those times with great affection, you know?"

Colette's words CHEERED Mousington. Suddenly, the producer knew what to do.

"Okay, you can play last," he told Colette.

"BUT BEFORE YOU GO, I HAVE A FAVOR TO ASK . . ."

LET'S BE FRIENDS

Meanwhile, Pam found Joel wandering around CAMPUS. When he spotted her, he looked more nervous than a mouse in a lion's den.

"Hey, Pam," he said hesitantly. "Are you still **mad** at me?"

Pam shot him her warmest smile. "I'm sorry, Joel! I was never mad at you. I just wanted you to understand how important my friends are to me. And I also want to say thanks for the song you wrote for us."

"Song?" the drummer asked, surprised. "What song? I haven't written anything in the last few days. My brain is already on vacation, and besides, I usually save my lyrics for the Ratstreet Boys."

Pam pulled out the lyric sheet and pawed

it to Joel. "Oh, you're sweeter than a cheese dumpling with syrup on top. Don't deny it! I'm sure you wrote these words."

The ratlet took the paper and read intently for a few moments. Then he stared at Pam curiously. "I wish I'd written something this good," he admitted. "It's a BEAUTIFUL song, and whoever wrote it must like you a lot."

You didn't write these lyrics?

Pamela **BLUSHED** and **LOOKED AWAY**.

"Now I understand why you don't want to come with me," he added. "It must be nice to have **FRIENDS** who appreciate you for who you truly are."

"I understand something, too," Pam replied, looking him in the eyes. "You and I are DIFFERENT, but that doesn't mean that we can't be friends."

Joel laughed. "You're really worth your weight in cheese, you know that?" He agreed to lend her his drum set for the tryouts.

When Pam returned to the auditorium, she found the other Thea Sisters waiting for her.

"You did it!" Violet cried as Colette **RAN** to hug her.

Nice work, Pam!

"We found new instruments," Nicky added. "We were just waiting for you!"

"Shhh, mouselets," Paulina hushed them as she poked her snout through the curtain's opening. "We're next!"

ONSTAGE, the second-to-last group was playing: the Ruby Crew!

The lights, the scene, the costumes, the musical arrangement, and even the prerecorded chorus were PERFECT, all thanks to the professionals that Ruby's mom had hired.

What wasn't working, however, were the voices of the four mouselets.

To make her squeak heard above the others, Ruby was screeching at the top of her lungs. The result was that she was completely **out of tune**!

Connie and Zoe realized what Ruby was doing, so they began WHISPERING. As for Alicia, she kept confusing the verses. To the trained ears of a producer like Mark Mousington, it was a total **DISASTER**!

When the music stopped, Mark jumped to his paws. "I am very impressed by your set design, mouselets."

Ruby smirked, convinced that she had aced the audition.

"But now I'd like to hear your song without the musical accompaniment," the producer went on. "I need to know if your voice is coming from your **HeaRt** or from the loudsqueaker!"

The Ruby Crew looked at one another, **terrified**.

Sing **WITHOUT** music?! They were absolutely **UNPREPARED** for this!

Ruby tried making up an excuse. She even asked the Ratstreet Boys for help, but they just shrugged.

Ruby's whiskers were wiggling with worry. Her eyes brimmed with tears. She didn't know what to do.

I just want to hear your voice!

Mark Mousington didn't seem to notice. "Your voice, Miss Flashyfur!" the producer concluded. "You just have to let me hear your natural VOICE."

Ruby decided to throw in the cheesecloth. All her classmates were there, and she had practiced so Little that she didn't want to embarrass herself by SINGING a cappella.

HER CAREER AS A ROCK STAR

WAS OVER BEFORE IT HAD EVEN BEGUN!

SUCCESS COMES FROM THE HEART

At last, it was the Thea Sisters' turn. They were nervous but *excited*.

As they took the stage, Pam told her friends what she'd learned from Joel: he hadn't written the lyrics. The songwriter's identity was still a secret!

Before they began **PLAYING**, Pam took Colette's microphone and made an announcement. "We dedicate this performance to the MYSTERIOUS songwriter who helped us. Whoever you are, thank you! You really helped make our dreams come true."

Ryder and Shen were the only ones at the **TRYOUTS** who knew the truth.

Ryder looked at Shen and winked.

Shen **PUT** his paw to his snout, asking Ryder to keep his secret. Maybe one day he would tell the truth. But not today, he thought. Today the spotlight should be on the Thea Sisters!

The mouselets began their act. Their hard work and practice paid off in a big way. Their performance was full of ENERGY, and Colette poured all her passion into her singing. The other mouselets really listened to one another's cues and played their instruments with gusto.

At the end of their performance, the crowd went wild. Shen, Elly, Ryder, and all the mouselets' friends were clapping **enthusiastically**.

Professor Ratyshnikov gave the Spice Mice

her highest **SCORE**. Even Bud, Jamal, and Raven from the Ratstreet Boys seemed **FRIENDLY** for once. They scurried over to praise the Thea Sisters' performance.

Professor Aria had a huge smile on her snout. She was so proud of her students' success.

But for the professor, the biggest **SURPRISE** was yet to come! While the audience was still applauding, a new **singer** joined the Spice Mice: **Mark Mousington**! He'd added one last number to the schedule. It was a song that would show Anna that nothing had changed between them, despite all the years of misunderstanding!

On Mark's request, Violet sat at the **KEYBOARD** and began playing the first notes of a sweet ballad.

Professor Aria felt like her heart was

about to **burst**. She immediately recognized the bars of "*The Road to Success*," the song she and Mark had never finished. Tears of **joy** began to run down her cheeks: Mark had completed their song, and he was singing it to her!

She rushed onstage to HUG her old friend, and he hugged her back. After so much time, they had finally forgiven each other!

They are so sweet!

"Oh, Mark!" Professor Aria sobbed. "I should never have LEFT our band!"

He smiled sweetly at her. "Anna, I didn't want to be the one to deprive you of your dream. That's why I didn't ask you to stay: you needed to be free to seize the moment!" He took her paw. "Anyway, it's all cheese under the wheel. Now the most important thing is that we're together."

The Thea Sisters began playing again, and the whole audience started dancing. So did Anna and Mark.

MiCE TAKE THE STAGE

At the end of the **AUDITIONS**, the judges agreed that the Spice Mice were the perfect choice to open for the Ratstreet Boys. Mark Mousington's team printed up flyers with the Ratstreet Boys' name in **BiG** letters. Underneath, in SMALLER LETTERS, was the name of the Spice Mice!

The **NIGHT** of the concert was magical for the mouselets. Before taking the stage, the five friends hugged one another tightly. This memory would live in their **HEARTS** forever.

"Let's rock, mouselets!" Nicky said.

"You said it, sis,"

Colette added, **WINKING** at Violet. "And let's have fun!"

Violet grinned at her. "After everything we've been through, this is what really counts: making *joyful music* for the audience!"

From their very first note, the Spice Mice commanded the crowd's attention. Their sound was bright and crisp, and their *energy flowed* from the stage like a river of cheese.

The crowd went wild. They sang and danced with the mouselets, filling the air with good vibrations. The Spice Mice wanted to stay onstage forever!

The Ratstreet Boys were so impressed with the Thea Sisters' performance that they called them back onstage for an encore.

It was a truly unforgettable night!

The day after the concert, Mark and the Ratstreet Boys had to leave. Pam and the other mouselets went to the heliport to see them off.

"Thanks for everything, Joel," said Pam, hugging her new *friend*. "Send me a postcard from your vacation, okay?"

"I will," he promised. "I hope I can come back and visit you sometime. Maybe I'll even go back to school myself one of these days."

Professor Aria and Mark Mousington said an affectionate good-bye and promised to chat every day.

Now that they had started listening to each other again, there was no distance that could keep them apart!

As they watched the big red helicopter fly away, the mouselets felt closer than

ever. They knew that true friendship could withstand any obstacle. It comes with us no matter what path we *choose*!

Don't miss any of these Mouseford Academy adventures!

#1 Drama at Mouseford

#2 The Missing Diary

#3 Mouselets in Danger

#4 Dance Challenge

#5 The Secret Invention

#6 A Mouseford Musical

#7 Mice Take the Stage

#8 A Fashionable Mystery

Don't miss any of these exciting Thea Sisters adventures!

Thea Stilton and the Dragon's Code

Thea Stilton and the Mountain of Fire

Thea Stilton and the Ghost of the Shipwreck

Thea Stilton and the Secret City

Thea Stilton and the Mystery in Paris

Thea Stilton and the Cherry Blossom Adventure

Thea Stilton and the Star Castaways

Thea Stilton: Big Trouble in the Big Apple

Thea Stilton and the Ice Treasure

Thea Stilton and the Secret of the Old Castle

Thea Stilton and the Blue Scarab Hunt

Thea Stilton and the Prince's Emerald

Thea Stilton and the Mystery on the Orient Express

Thea Stilton and the Dancing Shadows

Thea Stilton and the Legend of the Fire Flowers

Thea Stilton and the Spanish Dance Mission

Thea Stilton and the Journey to the Lion's Den

Thea Stilton and the Great Tulip Heist

Thea Stilton and the Chocolate Sabotage

Thea Stilton and the Missing Myth

Thea Stilton and the Lost Letters

Thea Stilton and the Tropical Treasure

Be sure to read all my fabumouse adventures!

#1 Lost Treasure of the Emerald Eye

#2 The Curse of the Cheese Pyramid

#3 Cat and Mouse in a Haunted House

#4 I'm Too Fond of My Fur!

#5 Four Mice Deep in the Jungle

#6 Paws Off, Cheddarface!

#7 Red Pizzas for a Blue Count

#8 Attack of the Bandit Cats

#9 A Fabumouse Vacation for Geronimo

#10 All Because of a Cup of Coffee

#11 It's Halloween, You 'Fraidy Mouse!

#12 Merry Christmas, Geronimo!

#13 The Phantom of the Subway

#14 The Temple of the Ruby of Fire

#15 The Mona Mousa Code

#16 A Cheese-Colored Camper

#17 Watch Your Whiskers, Stilton!

#18 Shipwreck on the Pirate Islands

#19 My Name Is Stilton, Geronimo Stilton

#20 Surf's Up, Geronimo!

#21 The Wild, Wild West | **#22 The Secret of Cacklefur Castle** | **A Christmas Tale** | **#23 Valentine's Day Disaster** | **#24 Field Trip to Niagara Falls**

#25 The Search for Sunken Treasure | **#26 The Mummy with No Name** | **#27 The Christmas Toy Factory** | **#28 Wedding Crasher** | **#29 Down and Out Down Under**

#30 The Mouse Island Marathon | **#31 The Mysterious Cheese Thief** | **Christmas Catastrophe** | **#32 Valley of the Giant Skeletons** | **#33 Geronimo and the Gold Medal Mystery**

#34 Geronimo Stilton, Secret Agent | **#35 A Very Merry Christmas** | **#36 Geronimo's Valentine** | **#37 The Race Across America** | **#38 A Fabumouse School Adventure**

#39 Singing Sensation | **#40 The Karate Mouse** | **#41 Mighty Mount Kilimanjaro** | **#42 The Peculiar Pumpkin Thief** | **#43 I'm Not a Supermouse!**

#44 The Giant
Diamond Robbery

#45 Save the White
Whale!

#46 The Haunted
Castle

#47 Run for the Hills,
Geronimo!

#48 The Mystery in
Venice

#49 The Way of
the Samurai

#50 This Hotel Is
Haunted!

#51 The Enormouse
Pearl Heist

#52 Mouse in Space!

#53 Rumble in
the Jungle

#54 Get into Gear,
Stilton!

#55 The Golden
Statue Plot

#56 Flight of the
Red Bandit

The Hunt for the
Golden Book

#57 The Stinky
Cheese Vacation

#58 The Super
Chef Contest

#59 Welcome to
Moldy Manor

The Hunt for the
Curious Cheese

#60 The Treasure of
Easter Island

#61 Mouse House
Hunter

#62 Mouse
Overboard!

*Don't miss
my journeys
through time!*

THE KINGDOM OF FANTASY

THE QUEST FOR PARADISE:
THE RETURN TO THE KINGDOM OF FANTASY

THE AMAZING VOYAGE:
THE THIRD ADVENTURE IN THE KINGDOM OF FANTASY

THE DRAGON PROPHECY:
THE FOURTH ADVENTURE IN THE KINGDOM OF FANTASY

THE VOLCANO OF FIRE:
THE FIFTH ADVENTURE IN THE KINGDOM OF FANTASY

THE SEARCH FOR TREASURE:
THE SIXTH ADVENTURE IN THE KINGDOM OF FANTASY

THE ENCHANTED CHARMS
THE SEVENTH ADVENTURE IN THE KINGDOM OF FANTASY

THE PHOENIX OF DESTINY:
AN EPIC KINGDOM OF FANTASY ADVENTURE

THEA STILTON: THE JOURNEY TO ATLANTIS

THEA STILTON: THE SECRET OF THE FAIRIES

THEA STILTON: THE SECRET OF THE SNOW

THEA STILTON: THE CLOUD CASTLE

WHALE ISLAND

MAP OF WHALE ISLAND

1. Falcon Peak
2. Observatory
3. Mount Landslide
4. Solar Energy Plant
5. Ram Plain
6. Very Windy Point
7. Turtle Beach
8. Beachy Beach
9. Mouseford Academy
10. Kneecap River
11. Mariner's Inn
12. Port
13. Squid House
14. Town Square
15. Butterfly Bay
16. Mussel Point
17. Lighthouse Cliff
18. Pelican Cliff
19. Nightingale Woods
20. Marine Biology Lab
21. Hawk Woods
22. Windy Grotto
23. Seal Grotto
24. Seagulls Bay
25. Seashell Beach

THANKS FOR READING,
AND GOOD-BYE UNTIL OUR
NEXT ADVENTURE!

Thea Sisters